HARRY SECOMBE'S
ZOO LOO BOOK

First published in Great Britain in 1999 by Robson Books, 10 Blenheim Court,
Brewery Road, London N7 9NT

A member of the Chrysalis Group plc

British Library Cataloguing in Publication Data
A Catalogue record for this title is available from the British Library

ISBN 1 86105 299 5

Printed and bound in Great Britain by
Butler & Tanner Ltd., London and Frome

HARRY SECOMBE'S

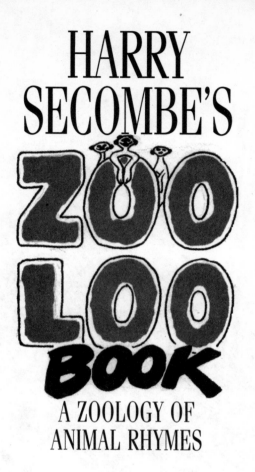

ZOO LOO BOOK

A ZOOLOGY OF ANIMAL RHYMES

ILLUSTRATED BY

BILL TIDY

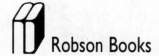
Robson Books

FOREWORD

When I was lying in bed recovering from a stroke, I found I had to keep my mind occupied. So I began to write these verses at the behest of Ronnie Cass, my musical director, who was writing some animal lyrics for children.

I sent him some limericks, but he said that they were a bit too sophisticated and suggested that I should do a book of them myself. We asked my old mate Bill Tidy to illustrate them and when he readily agreed, my cup runneth over. It's hard drinking with one hand!

Anyway folks, here they are and God bless all who sail in them.

Harry Secombe, September 1999

If a crocodile asks you to swim
Be extremely wary of him.
When you get in the water
Your legs will get shorter
Before you can say, "Hello Jim".

When taking tea at the zoo
Be careful, whatever you do,
Not to upset the camel,
That haughty old mammal,
By asking, "One lump or two?"

THREE, STOOPID, AND GET THOSE CHIMPS OUT OF HERE!
PLEASE DO NOT IRRITATE THE CAMEL
ZOO

"What do you give reindeer for Christmas?"
I hear all the Laplanders cry.
Six pairs of white silk pyjamas
To keep all his antlers dry.

ALL I EVER GET IS A PAIR OF BEARDSOCKS!

It's easy to baffle the wombat
Who lives in a hole in the ground.
Invite him to personal combat,
Or ask him for change of a pound.

"Aim between two lights like a giant
And stand tall and defiant,"
Said a crafty young toad
To a friend on the road
As towards them sped a Robin Reliant.

It's rare to find a bear without hair
'Cos he needs it to keep out the cold.
So if you should see a bear that is bare
It means he's got very old.

An orang-utan of Sumatra
Had a voice like the young Frank Sinatra.
He would flit through the trees
Without scratching his knees
Singing snatches from *La Traviata*.

A silly old bird is the bustard
Who lives on the African plains;
It only eats rhubarb and custard
And flies upside down when it rains.

BULK RHUBARB
AND CUSTARD

An agnostic hyena called Tim
Was always exceedingly grim.
When asked, "Where's your smiles?"
He said "I've got piles -
If you want me to laugh sing a hymn."

OH NO, NOT THE CHOIR OF CHALFONT ST. GILES!

Today I said, "Boo!" to a goose,
An action I don't recommend.
My knees are no longer of use
And my nose is all frayed at the end.

The Rhino is an ugly old thing,
His hide is tougher than leather.
But when it comes to the highland fling
His feet are as light as a feather.

LIMBERING UP
AREA

I'd like to praise the chimpanzee,
Some say he's our nearest relation.
He can swing by his toes
From any old tree,
Though I think I'll resist the temptation.

A mild-seeming monkey called Keith
Was exceedingly wild underneath.
He would hide in the loo
At Chessington Zoo,
And savage men's knees with
his teeth.

Betty Shepherd met a leopard
On her way to school.
Said Betty Shepherd to the leopard,
"How do you keep so cool?
You wear a fur coat all day long -
It surely makes you sweaty."
The leopard shook his head and smiled,
And swallowed little Betty.

OUT! YOU'VE ALREADY HAD ONE SCHOOL DINNER!

Never get cross with an albatross,
In the air he's the lord of all things.
No bird can deny that he is the boss,
For he can darken the sun with his wings.

"Y̶ou're looking quite pale,"
Said the grouse to the quail.
"What's happened that could be so drastic?"
"I'd a terrible fright last Saturday night -
I dreamt I was drowning in aspic."

Clarence, an amorous warthog,
Approached an old sow for a snog
Saying, "I'm ugly as sin -
And I'm no Errol Flynn -
But I look pretty good in a fog."

YOU LOOK EVEN
BETTER IN A BOG!

"They've gone off," said the hungry old fox,
Sniffing bones in a fried-chicken box.
"They're boilers in batter,
I think that's the matter.
On the whole, I prefer Plymouth Rocks."

"Forgive me for asking you this,"
Said an anxious young turkey from Diss,
"I've been invited to dinner
By someone called Winner -
Do you think I should give it a miss?"

An ostrich from far Zululand
Decided to form his own band.
But when he counted the beat,
They all had cold feet,
And buried their heads in the sand.

"Don't play with your food,"
Said the lynx to her brood
As they toyed with a spotted
    anteater.
"She's not very young, has a long
    sticky tongue,
And besides that, she knows you
    can't eat her."

As other rats fled in a panic
A lone rodent asked, "Why so manic?
It's really unthinkable -
This ship is unsinkable
Don't you know it's called the *Titanic*?"

"I don't give a hoot,"
Said the bald-headed coot
When invited to buy a toupee.
"I just couldn't care less
About being hairless.
I really quite like it this way."

In a shop full of china one day
Said a bull on refusing to pay
For the plates he had smashed,
"I am really abashed
But I don't carry cash, anyway."

"I'm the monarch of all I survey,"
Crowed the mouse on the table one day.
"I'll soon see to that,"
Said Whiskers the cat,
Who smiled as he put him away.

Misjudging a bend in the river,
A stork with a babe to deliver
Turned up in Westminster
At the home of a spinster,
Who called upon God to forgive her.

Said an edible frog from Versailles
As an epicure prodded her thailles,
"I've got horrible skin
And I'm awfully thin.
Besides that, I don't want to dailles."

"You're my dearest chum,"
Said the worm to his bum,
Quite unaware that his friend
Was his own rear end.
Still, sometimes it's best to be dumb.

JUST HOW DUMB CAN MY
NEXT MEAL GET?

A peke who was very petite,
Seeing a dachshund who lived in her street
Eating a sausage
He'd found in a passage,
Sniffed, "It's dog eating dog, so to speak."

"Just be calm and you'll come
   to no harm,"
Said the man at the crocodile
   farm.
"If they come any closer
Hit them right on the nose,
   sir."
Then I noticed he'd
   only one arm.

A swallow when nesting in Rome
To his mate said, "We ought to go home.
I think the hot weather's
No good for our feathers.
We'd be far better off in the Dome."

When failing to mate with a hat,
A mole who's blind as a bat
Said, "She can't be in season.
I think that's the reason
My lover has turned me down flat."

A performing giraffe named
  Alfredo
Had a trick which everyone
  loved so.
This clever young fella
Would swallow an umbrella
And regurgitate singing
  "Il mio tesoro".

"Don't ever try crossing this road,"
Said the friendly old frog to the toad.
"It's the M twenty-five
And you'll never survive.
You'd end up as flat as a board."

I NEVER REALISED HE WAS THAT TALL!

"I've a very large brain"
Bragged the Ugandan Crane,
"I don't think you'll find one that's faster.
I can count up to ten
And then back again."
Said the Booby "My God, you're a master!"

As its owner was scrubbing the floor
Her pet cougar shot through the door.
It slipped out of its tether,
Made a home in the heather,
And became known as
"The Beast of the Moor".

With her bosom all covered in gore
Cleopatra slumped to the floor.
Suppressing a titter
Said the asp as it bit her.
"They don't make 'em like this any more."

THOSE MELONS CAME IN HANDY FOR A DUMMY RUN!

The aardvark's shape is a funny one
And his expression is hardly a sunny one.
Though he lives in the wild,
He is really quite mild,
For aardvark never killed anyone.

A great-crested hornbill called Hewitt
Had a beak that resembled a cruet.
To make matters worse
And to add to the curse,
He got covered in salt when he blew it.

A short-sighted lion called Fred
Fell in love and decided to wed.
When he showed off his bride
To the rest of the pride,
They cried, "He's taken a Great Dane to bed!"

Said the mole to the hedgehog, "I'd date yer,
But I have to confess that I hate yer.
You take offence quickly
And you're always so prickly."
Said the hedgehog, "I guess that's my nature."

As around him his pals were all boisterous
A scared lemming said, "I'm quite anxious.
If they think it's a lark
To leap in the dark,
I don't - the idea's preposterous."

A transvestite hen from Malaya
Fell in love with a fowl who was gayer.
When they wanted to wed
All her catty friends said,
"She's not a cock - she's a layer."

When seeking to empty his bladder
A drunken man met with an adder.
He said, "Let's play a game,
Though I don't know your name.
All we need now is a ladder."

THIS IS NO TIME FOR PLAYING GAMES!

I say, have you heard
Of the Secretary Bird?
It's manners are really appalling.
It flies through the skies
Making arrogant cries
Such as, "What?" "Don't say that," and,
   "Who's calling?"

Percy the pub cockatoo
Would always turn the air blue.
"Hell and damnation,"
The landlord said in frustration,
And filled Percy's beak up with glue.

A chough on a bough said, "Heigh-Hough
I'm happy to be here, although
When the icy winds blough
And I'm covered in snough,
It's off to the Indies I'll gough."

A tiger in steamy Bengal
Took a walk through a big shopping mall.
He said with a sigh,
"If I wanted to buy,
There's no-one to serve me at all."

WHAT A DISAPPOINTMENT FOR THE TRUBSHAWE SEXTUPLETS!

The Jockey Club would not endorse
Plans to cross a giraffe with a horse.
They were far too high-tech.
Besides, the length of its neck
would beat every horse on
    the course.

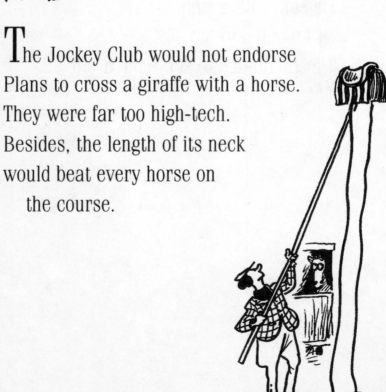

While entertaining his nieces
A chameleon who always loved wheezes
Said, "It's my great ambition
To crawl on a Titian."
So he did and burst into pieces.

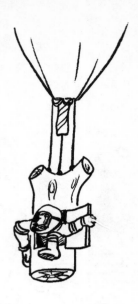

An astronaut-suited baboon
Escaped from a high-flying balloon.
He intercepted the flight
Of a meteorite.
Now it's raining baboon on the moon.

A disgruntled old tomcat named Vince
When hearing the word "nuts" he would wince,
For his own were cut off
When they asked him to cough,
And he hasn't caught sight of them since.